The Cloud Shack Gang

Published in the UK by Scholastic Education, 2022
Scholastic Distribution Centre, Bosworth Avenue, Tournament Fields, Warwick, CV34 6UQ
Scholastic Ireland, 89E Lagan Road, Dublin Industrial Estate, Glasnevin, Dublin, D11 HP5F

SCHOLASTIC and associated logos are trademarks and/or registered trademarks of Scholastic Inc.
www.scholastic.co.uk
© 2022 Scholastic
1 2 3 4 5 6 7 8 9   2 3 4 5 6 7 8 9 0 1

Printed by Ashford Colour Press
The book is made of materials from well-managed, FSC®-certified forests and other controlled sources.

A CIP catalogue record for this book is available from the British Library.

ISBN 978-0702-30913-7

All rights reserved. This book is sold subject to the condition that it shall not, by way of trade or otherwise, be lent, hired out or otherwise circulated in any form of binding or cover other than that in which it is published. No part of this publication may be reproduced, stored in a retrieval system, or transmitted in any form or by any other means (electronic, mechanical, photocopying, recording or otherwise) without prior written permission of Scholastic Limited.

Every effort has been made to trace copyright holders for the works reproduced in this publication, and the publishers apologise for any inadvertent omissions.

Author
Catherine Baker
Editorial team
Rachel Morgan, Vicki Yates, Fiona Undrill, Liz Evans
Design team
Dipa Mistry, Justin Hoffmann, Andrea Lewis, We Are Grace
Illustrations
Louise Redshaw/Plum Pudding Illustration

Help your child to read!

This book practises these letters and letter sounds.
Point and say the sounds with your child:

- ay (as in 'day')
- ou (as in 'out')
- oy (as in 'Troy')
- ea (as in 'each')
- ir (as in 'birds')

Your child may need help to read these common tricky words:

loved, the, he, of, all, by, was, someone, to, one, there, I'm, said, I, like, little, come, so, into, we, be, they

Before reading
- Look at the cover picture and read the title together. Read the back cover blurb to your child.
- Ask your child: *Have you ever seen a treehouse like this? Would you like to play in a treehouse?*

During reading
- If your child gets stuck on a word, remind them to sound it out and then blend the sounds to read the word: p-l-ay-i-ng, playing.
- If they are still stuck, show them how to read the word.
- Enjoy looking at the pictures together. Pause to talk about the story.

After reading
- Ask your child: *Whose idea was it to start the Cloud Shack Gang?*
- *How did Troy feel at the start of the story? How do you think he felt at the end?*

Troy loved his den in the treetops. He helped his dad construct it out of planks.

He painted it blue, all by himself.

Each weekend, Troy spent all day in the den.

But he wished he had someone to play with.

One Sunday, there was an odd sound underneath the den.

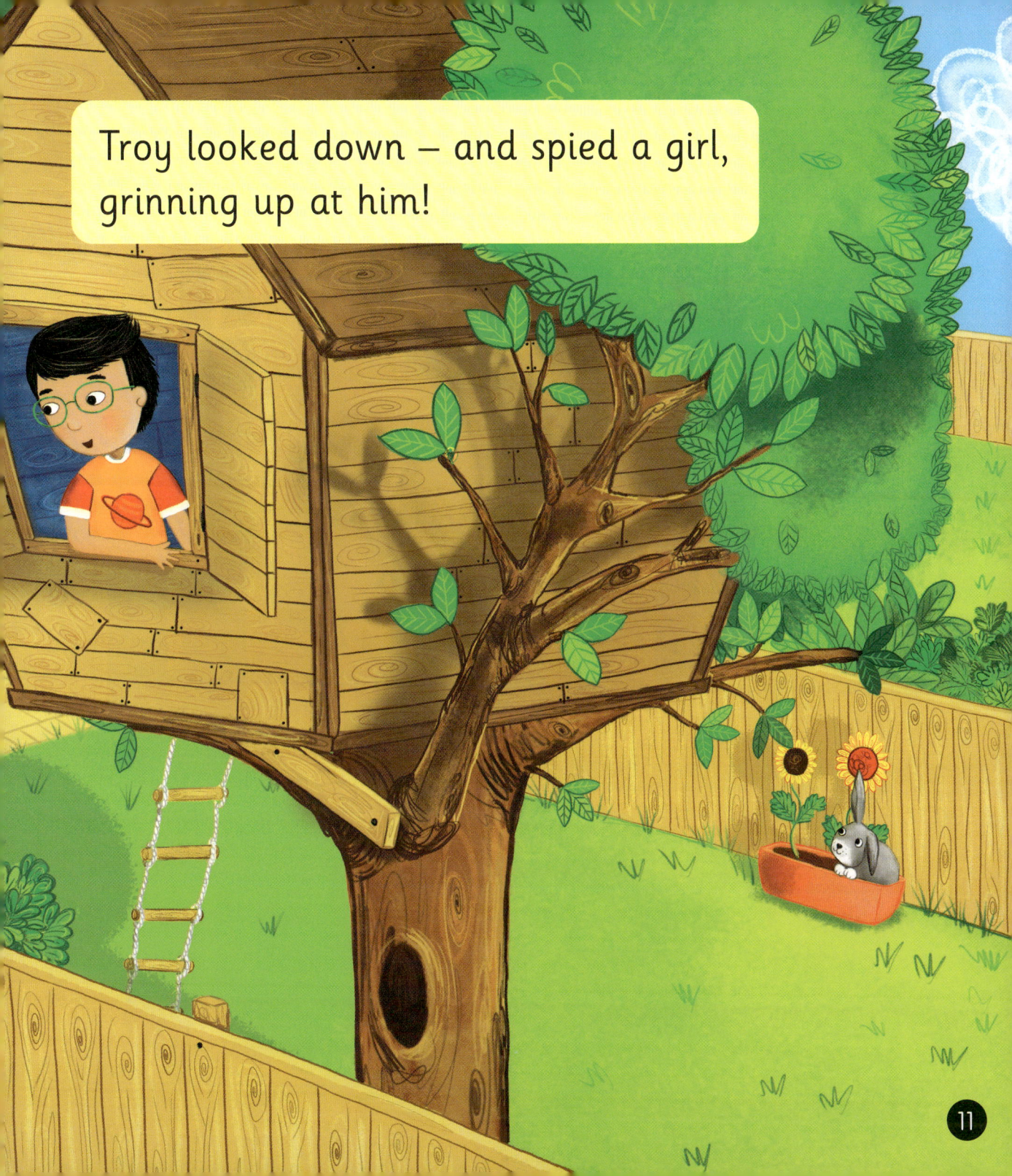

Troy looked down – and spied a girl, grinning up at him!

Troy grinned back at Sasha.
"Come and see it!" he shouted down.

So Sasha and her dad rang the bell.

Troy's mum took them round into the garden.

"Cool!" said Sasha, clambering into the den. "We can be the Cloud Shack Gang!"

Troy and Sasha spent the day painting a banner for the Cloud Shack.

They each found stuff for the Cloud Shack.

First, they added a toybox, then a unicorn blanket and a blue beanbag.

They tied up streamers and balloons.
It looked fantastic.

Retell the story